Where's my Turtle?

by Barbara Bottner

pictures by Brooke Boynton Hughes

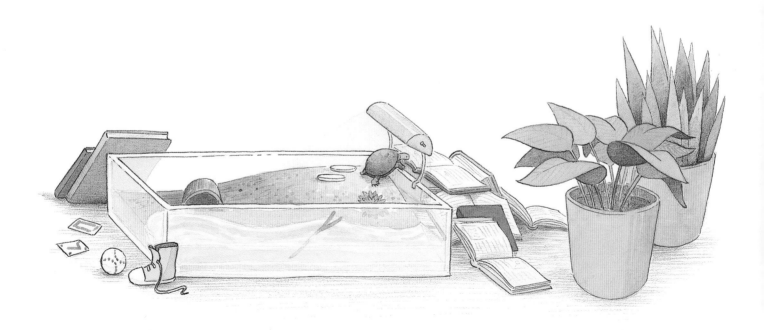

Random House ⌂ New York

Text copyright © 2020 by Barbara Bottner
Jacket art and interior illustrations copyright © 2020 by Brooke Boynton Hughes

All rights reserved. Published in the United States by Random House Children's Books,
a division of Penguin Random House LLC, New York.

Random House and the colophon are registered
trademarks of Penguin Random House LLC.

Visit us on the Web! rhcbooks.com

Educators and librarians, for a variety of teaching tools,
visit us at RHTeachersLibrarians.com

Library of Congress Cataloging-in-Publication Data is available upon request.
ISBN 978-1-5247-1805-3 (trade) — ISBN 978-1-5247-1806-0 (lib. bdg.) —
ISBN 978-1-5247-1807-7 (ebook)

MANUFACTURED IN CHINA
10 9 8 7 6 5 4 3 2 1
First Edition

Random House Children's Books supports the
First Amendment and celebrates the right to read.

For Gerald. At least we found each other.
—B.B.

For Tyler, Leah & Naomi
—B.B.H.

Archer lost things.

"What happened to my pens?"

"I can't find my truck!"

"Who took my baseball bat?" Archer cried.

"And where's Kevin?"

"A place for everything . . . ," Archer's mother began.

". . . and everything in its place," finished Archer.

"But I have to find Kevin.
What if he's hungry?
What if he's lost?"

He looked everywhere in his room.

But all he found was a blue truck.
"My blue truck! I *love* my blue truck!
It's my favorite!"

Archer played with his truck.
He heard something rustle.
"Kevin?" he called.

"If you put your toys away," said his mother,
"then it would be easier to find things—
especially things that can crawl away."

"Mom, what if Kevin's thirsty?"

"Have you looked outside?"

Archer looked everywhere in the yard.

All he found was his baseball bat.

"My baseball bat! I *love* my baseball bat!" said Archer.

"It's my favorite!"

Archer started practicing his hitting. But it was
not as much fun without Kevin watching.

"Maybe Kevin's hiding," said his mother.

"Hiding?" said Archer. "You mean scared to come out?"
Archer dug through every corner of the living room.
But all he found was his drawing pad and pens.

Art was Archer's favorite thing to do. He started
making a new drawing. But it was much more
fun when Kevin posed for a portrait.

"Mom, I *have* to find Kevin! He might be cold.
Or hot. Or hungry!"
"Remember what I told you?" his mother asked.

So Archer thought about "a place for everything,
and everything in its place."
He thought really hard.

Archer put his truck away
in the toy box.

He put his baseball hat
on a hook in his closet.

He gathered his drawings and pens
and put them neatly away in his desk.

Then, while he was at it, he put away his shoes,
his jacket,
      his pajamas,
            his baseball glove,
                  his books,
                        and all his puzzle pieces.

He stared at his clean, empty room.
"Mom, I put everything away,
but I still can't find Kevin!"

"*Think*, son," Archer's mom suggested.
"Think the way a *turtle* would think.
What would *you* do if you were Kevin?"

Archer thought. Then he got down on the floor.
He felt the shell on his back. He imagined he
was a small creature, lost, hungry, thirsty. . . .

Archer ran to the kitchen and poured
a glass of water into Kevin's bowl.

He took away Kevin's old food. He
found a banana, cut it into turtle-size
bites, and put them in Kevin's tank.

"Turtles like clean tanks!"
Archer wiped Kevin's tank until it was spotless.

Archer thought some more.
"And turtles *love* to be *warm*."
He opened the curtains wider
until sunshine filled the room.

Archer tried hard to keep thinking like
a turtle, but all he could think about
was how much he missed Kevin.

He slumped to the floor.
"Anything else turtles like?" his mother asked.

"I've got it—turtles like a *friend*!"
Archer whispered, "Kevin, I am your true and favorite friend.
And I miss you!"

"Please come back!"

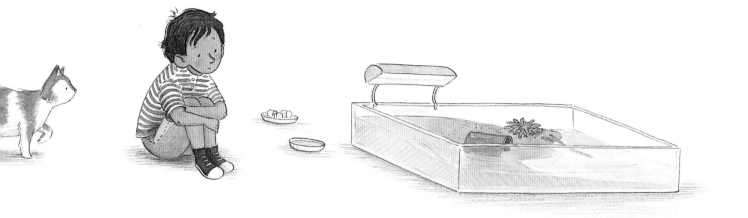

Archer waited . . .

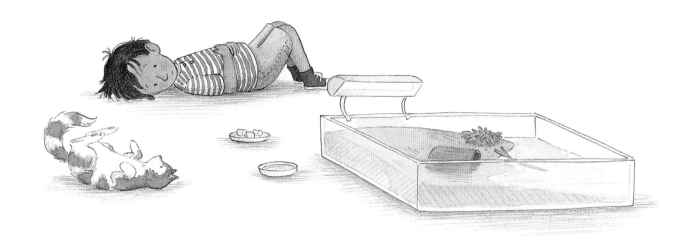

. . . and waited.

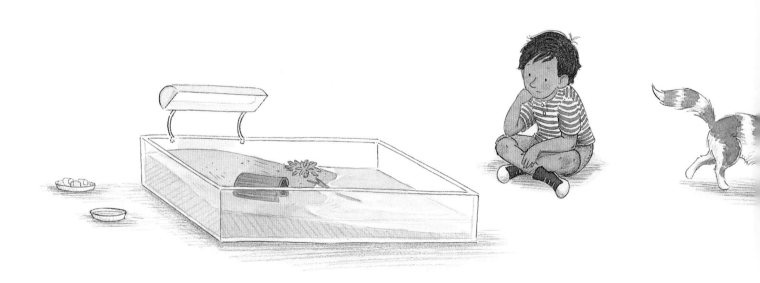

Then, from a dark corner, a tiny turtle crawled
slowly out into the sun, across the floor.

Kevin sipped some fresh water.
He nibbled on a turtle-size piece of banana.

Then he headed straight to Archer.

"Kevin!" cried Archer. "You're my absolute favorite thing of all!"